Low Rise

An escalation of microfiction from Dubai 2016

by

John F King

www.johnkinginternational.eu

ISBN 978-0-9931306-3-2

in Deira 2016.   photo credit: ADL

To

Angela, Dominic, Emilie, Fredric.

'…We were fond together because of the sweep of open places, the taste of Wide winds, the sunlight, and the hopes in which we worked…'

T E Lawrence

A Taste of Things

All I had on arrival in this country was my memory of food.

Mixing in the research — location, décor, music — the restaurant had to come out a success.

The first night was a dream. The second night dip didn't concern me. Third night the chef cooked her own dinner and left.

I blew the remaining budget on publicity — it could only be the missing ingredient.

When the phone rang I picked up first ring: 'Cedar Palace Restaurant'

I couldn't place the voice, sort of Deptford meets Deira —

'You been sending out these fliers..?'

Acquisitive Parker

4 minutes 27 seconds, put my feet down make it 4 minutes 12 seconds best. My front gate to Rashidiya station. Every day except Ramadan for countless years. Years are an obsolete metric. Station to my office top Jumeirah beach road 59 seconds.

I'm always the first there, checking everything out for the day. Nothing can ever go wrong. Some of the other operatives laugh at me, but I'm the one who is smiling. Only the best of the best for me.

First of the day, Tesla X. Could have seen it coming, glides beautifully, fraction too quiet for my taste. Next up, 007 all good boys go to heaven, Aston DB9. You can almost imagine the machine guns, girl in the ejector seat. Not that I'd want to, of course.

Things only move better, day goes on, fumes thicken, keys jangle. Lamborghini Aventador, handles like a wide awake dream. Parked in any space, 4 seconds.

Owner throws me the keys. I don't know where he goes, guess don't ask. Sir is the only name I know, never ask the ladies, rules are rules however unwritten.

Lunch is for losers. Every roar is a song. Bentley coupe takes up the most space, more is more, what a beauty. I'm on the best terms with the owner of that marque. Every thing is just so, I align it with the sidewalk – pavement as he calls it – never even needs to crease his suit.

Dusk is less old school, Berlinetta F12, Maserati Concept, even the Audi R8. Night clubs. I take a break, milk shake or coke zero by the road. Everyone looks at me, only the best for me, none of that dross the others get. Mr Reliable.

Gold class – what did you think – back to Rashidiya. Asleep in seconds. Dream. Speed back to Jumeirah. Mr Bentley throws me the keys. Look at the car, never the girl, the rule of rules. Later he returns from Trader Vics, different scent above the exhausts. He only spoke to me once –

'We'll walk,' he said, with a two second smile. I never saw him again, or her.

I'm still not sure what to do with the keys.

Gone with the Floe

It was always a treat to hear from Clarence. Good times, not so good times, his letters were always well written, black and white in content and style.

How long ago was it now since he set out? I remember his send off, how we all blubbed as he gave us a last wave from the horizon.

None of us had wanted him to go.

It was typical Clarence.

'One of us has to go,' he said in that gruff way of his, 'may as well be me.'

No one argued, you don't with natural authority. And with self-interest.

The ice was retreating visibly. We could never tell now if it was winter or summer. Food was scarce. Not everyone shared what there was as morale sank lower. It was time for action.

Clarence had volunteered for missions before. He was one of the few, those who had ventured beyond the horizon, and returned.

Only Clarence wrote, perhaps that is why he was always in the final selection for the reconnaissance missions. Others were chosen for a different set of skills, navigation, strength, contacts. Was he the only one who could write? The reports combining relevant facts with optimism. Things were scary enough without embellishment. It wasn't Clar's style to write if we don't find refuge by next summer it is the end of the species, Where would that get any of us? Or indulge in the black humour of some of the more muscular explorers like if we don't find ice soon what will you put in your drinks. It was all getting very thin.

Previous groups had voyaged due west and east, some were gone for a very long time. Clarence wrote of heroics in the high seas, waves that pushed you down forever or pushed you up to creatures on the surface, some friendly some not. Always factual, always positive but it was difficult to hide the unalterable fact behind any optimism false or otherwise – Clarence had not found a solution.

The letter indicated a change. It was most unusual for Clarence. He had permitted himself to investigate a rumour. A place to the north, a group of countries clustered around a warmer sea. Countries with black resources which gave them wealth to fulfil fantastical feats. Rumours of a dome, regulated, controlled. Rumours of some of our teams who had not returned had in fact not returned by choice. They had found a solution, a new life.

Clarence disliked rumour. To him everything was black and white. The deterioration of our situation and the persistence of the stories meant there was only one option. To find out, however arduous the journey, if it was true.

The letter confirmed it was.

In return for their sanctuary our fellow species had to perform entertainments which other species to use Clarence's term found amusing. They lived in a dome of permanent winter, of ice and cold water inside a building devoted to leisure and shopping activities they could only perceive beyond sheets of glass.

They could never leave the Dome. That was the deal. The environment beyond the Dome would kill you, but as Clarence weighed up so well in his epistle the environment we are in now, the one he left to explore, was dying too

The duties inside the dome seemed light, it wasn't a moment to think of dignity.

There is, said Clarence in the closing sentence of his letter, no alternative.

He was, he wrote in negotiation with the authorities of this fabled Emirate to supply him with a specially adapted machine to expedite his return and lead us on to the Dome. Clarence had found a way. Clarence was coming back.

He's So Shallow

It was the boss on the mobile.

-Would you mind coming in early today, he said. It wasn't a question. Tony the boss was English, it took me longer than most to realise his 'would you minds' or 'perhaps you'd like to' were orders as direct as any Emirates.

-Would you mind coming in early today, Sven can't go in.

-What's up, I said

-I'd be obliged if you'd come in, quick as you can. Appreciated, said Tony.

On site I learned that Sven had been warned, finally. Looking back I could have seen it coming, in this line of work if you don't go in, and in deep, there is nowhere left to go.

I was in the North Sea when I first heard about this job. I've always had a fear of being taken in by jokes. One of the divers from the Norwegian sector first told me about it. I never understood Norwegian humour. I discovered it was always best to listen when he told me stuff, work out if it was funny or not in the cabin later.

Sven told me through his mask mic about the job in Dubai. The water was black and almost freezing. We operated in a corridor of light from the helmet masks. He described a world of light and colour. I pointed to the surface with my gloved thumb.

Some things are best discussed top side.

As soon as he had the breathing mask off the words blew out of him.

-It's a dream, said Sven, I only wish I'd believed it when I first heard about it. The biggest aquarium in the world in the biggest shopping mall in the world. You go in twice a day, full gear, feed the fish, sharks, rays, angels, everything, make occasional demo with tourists or splash in at a private party. Everything supplied. Keep it under your helmet, don't want anyone applying for it. Best of the best only.

He stopped for a while. I thought he was catching his breath before I realised he was waiting for me to thank him. I hesitated.

-You want to stay here in the freezing dark? He said. I'm only telling you man. You're one of the best, you deserve a breather.

Sven had taken me out for a shore drink once when I told him I was separated from my family. No, I said, separated means you don't get to see them again, not as in after a rotation, but ever. I've never had the bends but I guess a shore night with Sven must be a close simulation.

-What is the downside, I said, too late. Sven was annoyed.

-I'm giving you a break man, he said, the fish aren't the only ones swimming in paradise.

When I looked up from the eye scanner at DXB there was a man sporting goggles in the Lexus pick up area. Not a bad joke for Sven.

We worked split shifts, he came out , I went in, vice versa next week. I learned from him. There were species I'd never seen before, you had to learn how to be around them. I asked Sven for advice – yeah, humans are pretty complex he said, they can turn on you if you don't feed them properly. He laughed first.

I loved the work. Arrive at the mall, digest a light lunch, briefing, change and into the blue. It was so peaceful. There was harmony in the light, every species getting along nicely. The shoals always so pleased to see me. I never looked out beyond the glass when I was working.

I'd settled in like a, well like a something in water, a natural habitat. The package included an apartment a few stops away on the metro. Sven smiled when I told him I came on public transport. Why don't you swim in he said, as he gave his Cayenne to one of the parkers.

It was a quite a while until we were both off together and out long enough to go for a drink. When I mentioned downside I thought Sven might have joked about swimming with rays but he looked at me seriously and said, the alcohol policy is a bit of a drag but there's always a way through the net.

I'd always enjoyed Sven's company, the small amounts of it he gave. Not everyone found a night out with Sven fun. Harder work than the deepest shift was the opinion of many. Perhaps it was that he and I talked the same amount that was the secret. To me he was quiet, withdrawn even, but himself. Said something when he had something to say, everything else was implied. Letting me in on the Dubai job was characteristic of his generosity.

We went to one of the hotel rooftop bars. -Time you saw this place from above, he remarked. He always drank neat, you might think he was afraid of something, but this was Sven. If it had stopped when it should have it would have been a nice evening. I looked at my watch for the first time about 11. - Time's up for me, I said. - I'll call it a night.

-We don't have to dive for another three days, he said -The night is so shallow.' -Young, I said -the night is still young. It was the first time, I reflected, I'd told him something he didn't already know.

There was an atmosphere that night that made me say - Look if you want to go on, we can, perhaps a late light supper, there's a new canal side restaurant I read about. Best fish in..

-I don't want to go to a restaurant, said Sven. -You go home, it's cool. See you, man.

I enjoyed the days off, Land Cruise to the desert, canal side restaurant with a girl from Edinburgh I'd met on the mall fashion walk.

When I reported back to the tank. Tony was there with two of the medical team next to Sven.

-He had a few drinks, went in before we'd assessed it, said Tony. -We can't have this. Isn't safe for anyone. I'm sorry but this isn't just going to be a dismissal but a deportation. I want an explanation. I mean you guys have everything going for you. Why did he do it? Isn't the first time. Talk to him.

Talk.

Littorally

I was pleased I wasn't dreaming. I hate dream homes. It was only when I awoke after my first night there I was confident it wasn't a dream. Really. The sea was there in front of the house, the house was there with me in it. I went upstairs to the main room, the vista was there, I was looking at it. Next door in my study I commuted to my desk with that view. On the surface the document was there – I owned the house. It was all true. Verifiable.

The intercom alert tone sounded. My interior designer. I trusted her completely. She had worked on my previous properties all over The World but I'd allowed myself to be palmed off with views of other people's fronds. I was looking forward to collaborating with Miranda on this, my first seafront home after all these tides.

-You are fortunate. Turquoise is totally in this season, opined Miranda.

-Make it happen, I ordered.

I emerged from my office to periodically look at the progress, the matching dining chairs, the DVD stacks, the chandelier, even the white goods became misnamed.

Miranda skyped the day after completion. We did a 360. It looks beautiful I said.

Next day the sea changed. I rang Miranda. Her phone was engaged.

Nothing is Everything

In this city where there is everything my job is nothing. It's rubbish. They drive, I cycle, they throw away, I collect, who do you think is happiest, closer to God, any of the gods represented here?

Everyday on my rounds I come across the most amazing things, the riches the rich throw away. I'm on my cycle from first light to evening prayers collecting, ordering. There is so much rubbish I return to the depot every hour to unload. What I see and find never ceases to astonish me.

Yesterday I found a speedometer from a Bugatti, a Hublot watch, a still-wrapped sandwich from Paul. I think it had meat in it. A Prada shirt with one button loose, an electronic map of a country I never knew existed. I empty my bin from the depot and cycle back to my designated area of the day. Some days I work beneath the world's tallest building, its shadow tells me time, some days I work by the marina, water, sky, glass lapping each other up.

I see all kinds of people, all kinds of things, new, what people call old but nothing in between. And always plastic, bottles, packaging, somethings I prefer not to mention.

I earn enough to send money home, there is no commission in my job but for me it is a kind of mission. I save and I save the earth. My boss has this joke — what do you want, a tip?

I smile. Why wouldn't I? Promotion for me was a new area, more responsibility, not somewhere new every hour, every day.

Some people see me, some don't — I see they are usually the ones who throw most away. I smile anyway. One man comes ashore from a boat each day. An hour later he returns to give things to his children. They look at his gifts through the plastic wrapping and discard them without opening them.

My job is to empty the bins. If I was here to make judgements I would have chosen another profession. I start a new area. I never knew if the man's presents were ever opened. I move on and never go back. Another area, there is even more rubbish, must be even richer than the zone I left. There is nothing new to speak of.

One day I heard a man and a woman arguing. I had seen them before, they seemed so at one, I was sorry to feel the raised voices, then the unpeaceful silence. In the beat of the sun I saw the man throw something in the bin. It had no plastic on it. When I emptied the bin it shone like nothing I had ever seen.

I hesitated. I wasn't sure if there was a category for recycling this item, perhaps it wasn't even technically rubbish at all.

It was a big risk, I could lose my job, but on instinct I cycled after the man now hazy in the distance.

I smiled, he didn't. I unfurled my gloved hand, the metal shone at any angle to the sun.

'Sir,' I said ' I think this is yours.'

'I think not,' he said before the smile met his eyes.

On Reflection

I'm still trying to figure it out, reality. The mega towers became ordinary skyscrapers, high rises became new flats, finally even the sub suburban villas melted into sand. I was on a narrow strip of tarmac. I'd unloaded my bicycle from the SUV beyond the Sheik Zayed road / DAMAC flyover.

It was my first solo ride after the event. I wasn't sure how I would feel back in the saddle . The only way to find out was to get back on it.

I thought I would be the one to ride out the cliché never lasts forever, things revert to ash or sand.

I'd never been out this way before. Our life was a city life, a waterside life, Dubai had defeated the desert, it was a beyond.

The guy on the 17th floor - Gareth, Gary, Garrick ? - had told me about the desert riders. Why would he make it up, this was a man who used the stairs. They met every Friday. I pictured him, point man with his group, their lurid shirts covered with logos, cycling into the sunset. Join us, he said, give you a new perspective, sweat it out.

Some other day, I said, we aren't really into that sort of thing.

He never asked me what we were into.

It was the first time in this city there wasn't a we. We had come out together, got our first apartment by the towers, our second by the beach, the third was too far. She went back to Surrey. I miss the green, she said. In my view she watched too many box sets.

We never could agree on the air conditioning settings.

When she left I never went out, selected my own season.

I was coming out of the lift on the 22nd floor one Sunday when the man who's name begins with G ran past. He was tanned and lithe and not even out of breath. I was ashamed of my pizzery weekend.

'What's the precise location? I asked him.

To be fair to G his group did their best to include me, they had sweepers to scoop up people like me. One Thursday I told him I'll ride solo, see them at the Bab al Shams for sundowners.

'Suit yourself, man' said G

As the group receded into the middle distance, the buildings merged with the sand. The camels legged past without giving me a second glance. I found peace again. I was pedalling at my own pace, there was a reachable destination, a defined horizon.

Then I saw her face, shimmering in the middle of the road rising before me.

Solar

'The person who follows the crowd will usually go no further than the crowd. The person who walks alone is likely to find himself in places no one has ever seen before.'

- Albert Einstein

I'd deployed the quote frequently, personally, in my coaching practice, whenever anyone could listen. I'd made a shedload in North America and Western Europe. Not that that was my motivation. On the contrary. The money came because I did what I wanted more than competently. And facilitated others to help themselves.

Coaching here was only moderately successful. Was I ahead of my time or was it a cultural difference? Some people don't like not being told what to do.

I couldn't buy as big a boat as I visualised. Then I figured big was for others, it wasn't me. As long as I was afloat it felt good.

People stared at my boat from the Uber Yacht parties departing the Yacht Club pontoons. The stares melted to laughter. You wouldn't call my boat flash, the parties on my prow would be extremely select – and not because I don't have many friends - I do.

On the days off I allocated myself I checked the roof panels. They were always fully charged. It was a life without clouds. I was happy sailing round the marina, out to sea past The Palm, the mega yachts moored beyond the One and Only. The panels lasted for a full day out. I returned as the sun set, charged up for another day.

I asked one of my clients who worked in marketing to design a logo for the hull. It was payment in kind. She had temporarily fallen adrift due to the non-renewal of a contract. Something to do with 'culturally inappropriate behaviour' in the Barasti at an after boat product launch. It isn't my business to judge.

The logo looked outstanding on the side of the boat. Business surged. I hadn't time to go sailing. The panels maxed out in the summer – or is that winter – months.

I returned to the marina in October. The panels in the charge took me further than I'd ever been before. I moored the far side of The Palm.

There were glints on the horizon. I peered through the binoculars. A flotilla of boats silently coming towards me, panels catching the sinking sun. The air horns broke the stillness.

How did that quote go — Hitchens was it? —

'What is your idea of earthly happiness? To be vindicated in your own lifetime.'

Not that I was searching for it.

www.johnkinginternational.eu 2016 Low Rise / Solar~

The Sun and Dirham

DAX, LSE, MICEX, DIFC , you want me to go on? Timing is everything, when to sell, when to buy, when to stop, when to start.

I'd made enough noise to live quietly. Unusually for me then I found the idea in a hardback but I hadn't found the place in my head or in the world.

I'd only been this far out of town once before buying gold, the best in the region.

When I came back to Deira I got lost in the maze but that is how I found it.

I gave the owner of the Bastakia house the asking price, I'd had enough haggle for a lifetime.

My days were low key, setting up the workspace, finding myself again the priority.

It was some time before I welcomed people in, they could watch me work, chat if they wished, I wasn't selling.

Mostly landscapes before I could face portraits.

I painted your portrait from memory, the photos were all up the creek.

A man came in to the studio space, looked and left in silence, came back a few days later when I'd made three more strokes.

'How much is it?' he inquired his stare never leaving the canvas. Did I recognize him?

'I'm glad you like it. This one isn't for sale.' I replied.

'I didn't say I liked it, I said how much is it.'

I repeated my answer. He repeated his question or was it a statement?

'Name your price.'

Low Rise 2016

ISBN 978-0-9931306-3-2

Low Rise

2016

Low Rise~

Top Job

From where I'm sitting it's the best job in the Gulf. Not everyone agrees with me - construction can be a competitive business. For some people it's the architect, without her they say there is nothing. For others it's the bricklayers, making it happen step by step. Some say it's the electricians, their wires like spinal cords up the lengthening shafts. But I am, indisputably, at the top, in my crane cab, master of all I survey, everything beneath me. In the distance I can see 7 countries, the sea, the desert. The building below rises to meet me, but it never actually can.

It isn't my name but the names of the construction company - Halvard Soulness printed into the crane shaft. At night I can see their names shining over our huts. One night I saw the bulbs making out the U were out. I reported it to the foreman. They were fixed within the hour. I was so impressed.

The site is like the United Nations, the Scandinavian owners, the Emirates money, the engineers from Holland, the surveyors from England. Everything fits. German welders put the plates together and compatriot bargemen push them in from the ocean up the marina onto my hook. I wind them up to the top. The dots below me fix them. Indian lifting experts put inserts into my crane to keep me always at the highest point. Each day my journey to work gets longer but the view excels.

On Saturday I lower my cab to umpire our cricket match, Bangladesh v Rest of the World – it isn't the Ring of Fire but I'm impartial.

Naturally the day must come when my job ends. I wasn't, yet, an astronaut. I will return to earth and start to work my way up again. The build felt and looked complete. The only way was down. I was so proud. I was in the highest crane on earth.

I was surprised when the order came to continue in my work. I hoisted up another satellite antennae, a weather beacon, yet more aircraft lights.

On handover night on Halvard Soulness arranged for us to watch Al Jazeera. The mood in our hut was celebratory , we passed round Mithai. The theme tune to the documentary began, then the bold titles, World's Tallest Building.

Then the silence. The building wasn't our clients, it was in a country so faraway I couldn't even see it from my cab.

That evening the foreman told me to report back to the site at first light next day to continue my work. Apparatus was laid out before my hook like fish at Swarighat market. A fire beacon, aircraft – or satellite - warning lights, a new coms antennae. The surveyors from London measured them meticulously and conferred. Then the order came. I lifted them, higher, and higher and still higher..

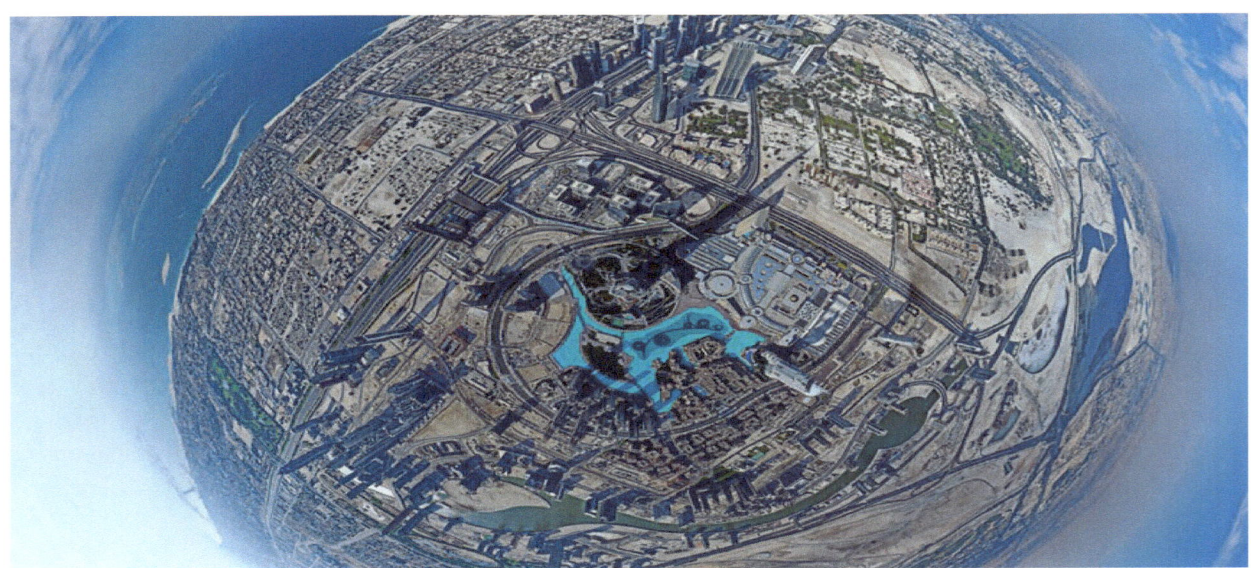

The Windows of the Soul

I've worked at DXB all my life. Security. I've never been anywhere else but I've seen everything. Nothing gets past me. I'm infallible.

I'm the way into this city. If I'm programmed to think you're trouble you'll never get in to make it. Don't even think about trying to scam past me, I won't allow it. Trust me.

I receive a constant stream of information. As soon as you arrive you look into me, if you match anything I know I alert my masters.

Most people I look on benignly. Their smile reaches their eyes. They are here to see people they love, to have fun, to work, to live in a certain way. That doesn't concern me. I don't have a view on that. Personally.

I never sleep, not a wink, I am always looking, I will always see you. I know more about you than you do but you will never see me. Again.

Imagine a life without goodbyes.

Visual Construct

Visual Remembered

Auditory Construct

Auditory Remembered

Feelings

Self Talk

GATE   SEAT

\-   **83D**

DUBAI

DXB

MANCHESTER

MAN

DEPARTS
28 Apr, 14:35

ZONE
C

FLIGHT
EK019

TIER
Blue

PASSENGER
John King

SEQ
361

CLASS
Economy

ⓘ

Low Rise

John F King

ISBN 978-0-9931306-3-2

York Europe Publishing

www.johnkinginternational.eu

2016

Also by **John F King** at **York Europe Publishing:**

<u>Wise Guy and other fables</u>, 2008

ISBN 978-0-955851902

      <u>Wise Guy,</u> 2012, is also available as an eBook at

Smashwords ISBN 9781476351735

*<u>Drama King</u>, 2010

ISBN 978-0-955851919

<u>Funky / Guy and other micro-fiction</u>, 2012

ISBN 978-0-955851964

<u>Micro-Waves</u>, 2012

ISBN 978-0-955851933

<u>Vienna, Love,</u> 2014

ISBN 978-0-955851971

<u>Write Coach,</u> 2014

ISBN 978-0-955851988

<u>Write Coach</u> II 2015

ISBN 978-0-9931306-1-8

<u>A and E</u>   2014

ISBN 978-0-955851995

<u>Prog</u> 2015

ISBN 978-0-9931306-0-1

<u>What's Left</u> 2016

ISBN 978-0-993106-2-5

John F King has completed creative writing courses at

Artworks

Arvon

City Lit London

JBW London

Oxford University Department for Continuing Education

Script Yorkshire

Skyros Writers' Lab

UCLA (online), UEA / Future Learn (online)

York University Centre for Lifelong Learning

/Low Rise 2016

www.ingramcontent.com/pod-product-compliance
Lightning Source LLC
Chambersburg PA
CBHW041541240626
47164CB00002B/85